D1636890

IT'S WEIRD. ALL THIS JUNK AND THE JOKER TAKES ONLY ONE LOUSY STATUE.

ESPECIALLY SINCE WORD ON THE STREET SAYS HE'S DESPERATE FOR CASH THESE DAYS.

THINGS ARE NEVER WHAT THEY SEEM WITH THE JOKER.

I GUESS THE NIGHT BRINGS OUT ALL THE WACKOS!

THE STATUE WAS MADE OF JADE. WORTH MAYBE A HUNDRED GRAND.

I'D LIKE A CLOSER LOOK.

HEY! HE CAN'T LEAVE A CRIME SCENE WITH EVIDENCE!

YOU WANT TO STOP HIM, BE MY GUEST.

OKAY, FREAK! HAND IT...

AW, NUTS!

HOW DOES HE DO THAT?

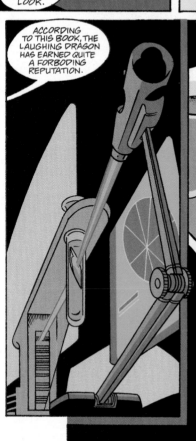

ACCORDING TO THIS BOOK, THE LAUGHING DRAGON HAS EARNED QUITE A FORBODING REPUTATION.

EVER SINCE IT WAS CARVED IN CHINA NEARLY THIRTY YEARS AGO, IT HAS PASSED THROUGH SEVERAL OWNERS, ALL OF WHOM DIED PREMATURELY.

-5-

-7-

YAAAAA!

I HOPE I DIDN'T SHAKE YOU AND THE OTHERS UP TOO BADLY, LOIS.

... JUST HAPPY I COULD HELP OUT, MR. PRESIDENT.

I HATE TO ADMIT, I'VE GOTTEN USED TO IT.

UH, SUPERMAN?

YES?

AH, HOW CAN I PUT THIS?

I WAS JUST THINKING... IT MIGHT BE NICE TO SEE EACH OTHER WHEN I WASN'T, I DUNNO, FALLING OUT A WINDOW OR SOMETHING.

NOT THAT I'M NOT GRATEFUL FOR ALL THE TIMES YOU'VE HELPED ME, YOU UNDERSTAND...

I UNDERSTAND.

YOU DO?

BANG BANG SCREEEE

THAT'S THE FIRST NATIONAL BANK.

...OKER.

I CAN'T BELIEVE YOU RECOGNIZE ME! HOW FLATTERING!

LEXY, OLD KID, DO I HAVE A DEAL FOR YOU!

I DON'T MAKE DEALS WITH MADMEN.

LEX, LEX! IS THAT ANY WAY TO SPEAK TO A KINDRED SPIRIT? OH, THERE ARE DIFFERENCES TO BE SURE...

...LIKE HAIR! HA!

WHAT DO YOU WANT?!

IT'S LIKE THIS. THANKS TO THAT MISERABLE, POINTY-EARED RODENT, BATMAN, ALL MY OPERATIONS IN GOTHAM CITY HAVE BEEN SHUT DOWN.

MY HEART BLEEDS FOR YOU.

AHH! BUT YOU, TOO, HAVE AN OVERGROWN BULLY IN LONG UNDERWEAR, WHICH BRINGS ME TO MY LITTLE PROPOSITION.

I'M LISTENING.

PAY ME ONE BILLION DOLLARS, AND I'LL KILL SUPERMAN.

WHAT MAKES YOU THINK YOU CAN KILL SUPERMAN WHEN YOU CAN'T EVEN HANDLE A MERE MORTAL IN A HALLOWEEN COSTUME?

THERE'S NOTHING MERE ABOUT THAT MORTAL!

BESIDES, I'VE READ UP ON YOUR FLYBOY. I KNOW HIS WEAKNESS! SEE?

SOLID KRYPTONITE!

YOU KNOW I CAN'T BE CONNECTED TO THIS IN ANY WAY.

YOU'LL BE MR. CLEAN, I PROMISE. DEAL?

DEAL.

LEXCORP
ANDING FIELD
RIVATE

I HEAR WAYNE'S DEAL WITH LEXCORP COULD RUN INTO THE BILLIONS. HE'S A HIGH ROLLER.

I HEAR HE'S NOTHING BUT GOTHAM TRASH.

RICH, SPOILED...

-13-

NOT CLOWN... JOKER!

Gulp!

SHING

I'M IN TOWN ON BUSINESS AND NEED A PLACE TO HANG MY HAT. LIKE YOUR PLACE.

ARE YOU NUTS?

KILL HIM!

Ooof!

Urrg!

OOH! CAN I PLAY, TOO?

CARLINI, ALL THAT SPICY FOOD-- YOU LOOK A LITTLE GASSY!

NO! STOP!

Cough! cough!

SSSSS

Heh Heh

HA HA HA HA HA HA HA

HOLY GUACAMOLE! LOOKS LIKE YOU BOYS ARE GOING TO NEED A NEW LEADER!

HA HA HA HA HA

WELL, I'M PROUD OF THE WORK *BOTH* OUR TEAMS HAVE DONE. THESE ROBOTS ARE GOING TO REVOLUTIONIZE UNMANNED SPACE TRAVEL.

ACTUALLY, THERE MAY BE A USE FOR THEM CLOSER TO HOME.

THE JOINT CHIEFS HAVE SHOWN TREMENDOUS INTEREST. IT DOESN'T TAKE MUCH IMAGINATION TO ENVISION THESE ROBOTS ON THE BATTLEFIELD.

EXCEPT, I WON'T ALLOW IT.

WHAT?

I DON'T LIKE GUNS.

WELL, BRUCE, I THINK I HAVE SOMETHING TO SAY ABOUT THIS...,

NOT ACCORDING TO OUR DEAL. ALL TECHNOLOGICAL APPLICATIONS NEED MY APPROVAL FIRST.

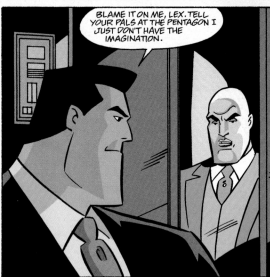

BLAME IT ON ME, LEX. TELL YOUR PALS AT THE PENTAGON I JUST DON'T HAVE THE IMAGINATION.

SO HE JUST APPEARS WHEN THERE'S TROUBLE? NO SPECIAL SIGNAL?

HE'S NOT LIKE YOUR BATMAN, THANK GOODNESS.

SO HOW DO YOU GET IN TOUCH WITH HIM?

COMMITTING A FELONY HELPS. LISTEN, YOU SEEM AWFULLY INTERESTED IN SUPERMAN. DO YOU WANT ME TO FIX YOU TWO UP?

SORRY.

NO, I'M SORRY. IT'S JUST THAT I'VE BEEN A LITTLE TOO CONSUMED WITH THE MAN OF STEEL LATELY.

MAYBE WE COULD CHANGE SUBJECTS.

NO MORE MEN IN TIGHTS?

DEAL.

A FEW NIGHTS LATER...

SO JUST KEEP YOUR EARS OPEN, BIBBO. LET ME KNOW IF YOU HEAR ANY BUZZ ABOUT THE JOKER.

SURE THING, MR. KENT. BUT, UH, WHICH ONE?

THERE'S LOTSA JOKERS AROUND HERE.

HEY, SWEETHEART!

WHAT ARE YA, DEAF?

I SAID ANOTHER... AHHHH!

IT'S BEEN A LONG TIME, BINKO.

I HEARD YOUR BOSS CARLINI'S BEEN REPLACED BY THE JOKER. WHERE IS HE?

WHO KNOWS? MAKIN' HA-HA WITH HARLEY QUINN.

I-I-I-I DON'T KNOW, HONEST! I NEVER WENT BACK AFTER HE MUSCLED IN. I DON'T WANT NOTHIN' TO DO WITH THAT CLOWN!

THAT'S ENOUGH.

I THINK YOU GOT YOUR ANSWER.

YAAA!

HELLO?

HI.

I JUST WANTED TO LET YOU KNOW, I'LL BE IN LATE TOMORROW. I'M HAVING BREAKFAST WITH BRUCE.

ISN'T THAT SPECIAL.

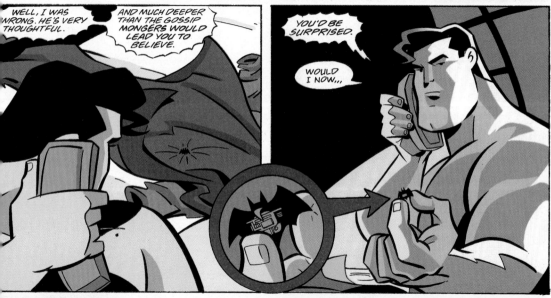

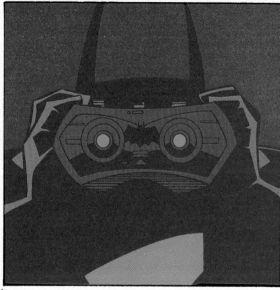

TOUCHÉ.

KRUSH

THE...SEN...ATOR... DE...CLINED..,COMMENT.

DONE!

AND NOT A MINUTE TOO SOON.

BRUCE?! WHEN DID YOU...?

ABOUT TEN MINUTES AGO. I DIDN'T WANT TO DISTRACT YOU.

GIVE ME A MINUTE TO SEE THE CHIEF. THEN I'M ALL YOURS.

CLARK, KEEP AN EYE ON BRUCE, WILL YOU?

ACTUALLY, LOIS...

SHE NEVER STOPS, DOES SHE?

NOT THAT I'VE NOTICED.

ANY LUCK FINDING THE COMEDIAN?

IT'S BEEN THREE NIGHTS AND NOT SO MUCH AS A GREEN HAIR.

OF COURSE, YOU HAVE BEEN DIVIDING YOUR TIME BETWEEN WORK AND LOIS.

IS THAT A PROBLEM?

LET'S JUST SAY I'M CONCERNED.

YOUR REPUTATION IS-- DUBIOUS.

IN AND OUT OF COSTUME.

DON'T WORRY. I'M TAKING LOIS QUITE SERIOUSLY.

BESIDES, IT SEEMS TO ME YOU HAD YOUR CHANCE.

BE SEEING YOU.

THIS CITY IS BEAUTIFUL AT NIGHT.

IS IT? I WASN'T LOOKING AT THE CITY.

LOIS, ABOUT CLARK KENT. ARE YOU AND HE... I MEAN...?

AIR JOKER, NOW BOARDING AT GATE ZERO!

WELL! AREN'T WE TENACIOUS?

CATCH YOU NEXT TIME, BRUCIE! HA, HA, HA!

SWELL. NOW GOTHAM'S SENDING US THEIR WACKOS.

DON'T WORRY, MR. WAYNE. THE *SCU* WILL GET HER BACK SAFE AND SOUND.

THANK YOU, INSPECTOR TURPIN.

YOU REALIZE SHE'S JUST THE BAIT.

I'LL BE CAREFUL.

"CAREFUL" WON'T CUT IT. WITH JOKER, EXPECT THE UNEXPECTED.

MAYBE YOU SHOULD HAVE REMEMBERED THAT.

I SENSE A CERTAIN TENSION BETWEEN YOU AND SUPERMAN, SIR. DO YOU QUESTION HIS CAPABILITIES?

NO. JUST HIS JUDGMENT. HE DOESN'T GRASP THE LIMITS OF BRUTE STRENGTH AGAINST A MIND AS WARPED AS THE JOKER'S.

MIGHT I SUGGEST KEEPING A COLLEGIAL EYE ON HIM?

EXACTLY WHAT I HAD IN MIND.

THINK OF IT, MISS LANE!

THIS ROCK IS MORE PRECIOUS THAN GOLD! ONE TEENSY CHIP WILL GO FOR THOUSANDS ON THE COLLECTOR'S MARKET...

...AFTER IT KILLS YOUR FLYBOY!

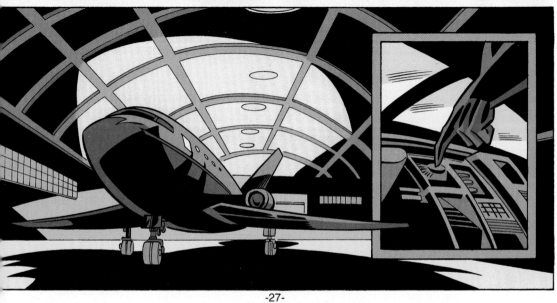

TURPIN WASN'T HAPPY I WOULDN'T TELL HIM THE JOKER'S LOCATION--

-- BUT WHEN THAT MADMAN CALLED, HE PROMISED LOIS WOULD DIE LAUGHING IF I DIDN'T COME ALONE.

MORE POWERFUL THAN A LOCOMOTIVE--AND JUST ABOUT AS SUBTLE!

WHERE IS SHE, JOKER?

MMMUMMMFF!

HA, HA, HA, HA!

HISSSS

HISSSS

TWO HEROES FOR THE PRICE OF ONE! I LOVE IT!

AND THE BEST PART IS...

YOU'RE ALL GOING OUT ON A SMILE!

HAVE A HAPPY!

KRESH

...THERE...!

HYDROCHLORIC ACID? IT WOULD TAKE A WEEK TO EAT THROUGH THAT DOOR.

NO... USE ON KRIH...

HCL

SNAP OUT OF IT, KENT--OR JOKER GETS THE LAST LAUGH.

KEEP YOUR HEADS DOWN.

CLANGS

THEY'RE LOOSE!

NO FAIR!

IT'S OVER, JOKER.

IT HASN'T EVEN BEGUN, SUPIE!

MARBLES?

THEY'RE GRENADES!

EXPECT THE UNEXPECTED.

BOOM
BOOM
BOOM

THANK YOU. I COULDN'T HAVE SAVED LOIS WITHOUT YOUR HELP.

I'M AWARE OF THAT.

BRUCE! BRUCE WAYNE! HE WAS WITH ME WHEN THE JOKER--IS HE ALL RIGHT? DO YOU KNOW?

HE'S FINE. JUST FINE.

WHY DID THE JOKER DO THIS?

WHAT'S HE DOING IN METROPOLIS?

ANY COMMENTS, MR. LUTHOR?

SHOW'S OVER, BOYS. PACK IT IN.

WHAT COULD HAVE POSSESSED ME TO TRUST THAT CLOWN?

HELLO, MR. J! I'M BATMAN! EAT ME! EAT ME! EAT ME!

Sigh...

I KNOW YOU'RE TRYING TO CHEER ME UP, HARLEY. BUT, YOU SEE, ANYTIME I BLOW A BILLION-DOLLAR DEAL...

...IT REALLY KILLS MY APPETITE!

Eeek!

HONESTLY, LEX, DON'T YOU THINK I FEEL BAD ENOUGH ALREADY?

YOU MANIAC! YOU IDIOT! HOW DARE YOU USE ONE OF MY LABORATORIES...

H-H-HARLEY?

PUT HIM DOWN, BALDY!

MERCY!

HERE'S FOR THAT RIDE IN THE TRUNK!

Unngh!

OOOH! LISTEN TO LITTLE MISS CAN'T-TAKE-A-JOKE!

CAN'T WE DISCUSS THIS LIKE GENTLEMEN?

AHHH!

BANZAI!

YOU OWE ME AN EXPLANATION.

THE LAB WAS A PERFECT SETUP. HOW DID I KNOW OLD BAT-BREATH WOULD SHOW UP?!

BATMAN? HE FOLLOWED YOU TO METROPOLIS?

OH, RIGHT! LIKE IT'S MY FAULT!

UNNGH! OOOF! OWW!

OH, WAS THAT YOUR FACE? I'M SORRY!

LOOK, I'VE STILL GOT HALF THE KRYPTONITE. I CAN STILL FINISH THE JOB...

UNACCEPTABLE. IF YOU CAN'T HANDLE SOME MENTAL CASE IN A FRIGHT MASK, OUR DEAL IS OFF.

MERCY...

I!!!!

LET'S GO.

KEEP IN MIND, THIS IS YOUR LAST CHANCE.

HOW YA DOING, SLUGGER?

...A-OKAY, MR. J.!...

GOOD GIRL.

...*!

SLAP!

HEY, SMALLVILLE! WHAT'S UP?

I SEE YOU'VE BEEN HOLDING UP AFTER LAST NIGHT. I'VE BEEN --OH.

I DIDN'T REALIZE YOU HAD COMPANY.

HOLD ON, KENT. YOU MIGHT AT LEAST TELL US WHY YOU STOPPED BY.

I'VE BEEN NOSING AROUND. I THINK I KNOW WHY THE JOKER IS SUDDENLY AFTER SUPERMAN.

I THINK HE'S IN CAHOOTS WITH YOUR BOYFRIEND'S BUSINESS PARTNER.

LEX WORKING WITH THE JOKER? ARE YOU SURE?

I CAN'T PROVE IT. YET.

I SUPPOSE I COULD ASK HIM.

WH- WHAT? WHO...?

AHH!

WHAT DO YOU WANT?

INFORMATION. REGARDING A MUTUAL ACQUAINTANCE.

WHAT ARE YOU TALKING ABOUT? I DON'T KNOW ANY...

YOU KNOW EXACTLY WHO I MEAN. WHERE IS HE? WHAT KIND OF DEAL HAVE YOU MADE WITH HIM?

Unghh!

ALFRED, HOW FAST CAN WE GET TO HOBBS BAY?

LAFF NIGHT AT HOBBS BAY

IF I MAY BE SO BOLD, WHEN IN ROME, SIR...

WHAT'S THE PROBLEM, CAPTAIN?

WHAT DO YOU MEAN?

YOU SENT OUT A DISTRESS CALL, DIDN'T YOU?

NOT ON MY AUTHORIZATION!

WAIT...

THERE'S THE CULPRIT. IT'S BROADCASTING AN ELECTRONIC BEACON.

IF ONE OF MY CREW IS RESPONSIBLE FOR THIS PRANK, I'LL--

WHAT IS IT? WHAT'S HAPPENING?!

WHOEVER SENT THAT DISTRESS SIGNAL... JUST PROVIDED THE DISTRESS!

COPY-BAT! COPY-BAT!

SUFFERING FROM PROPULSION ENVY, BATBOY?

TARGET IDENTIFIED

BEFORE YOU SLAP ME SILLY, THERE'S SOMETHING I'D LIKE YOU TO SEE...

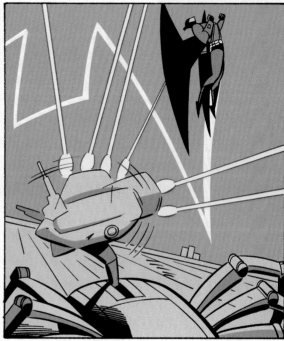

unngh!

NO!

ERGENCY

BRUCE?!

SO, WHEN WERE YOU GOING TO TELL ME? THE HONEYMOON?

LOIS...

STAY BACK!

DID I MISS ANYTHING?

HE SURVIVED. HE LASTED LONG ENOUGH FOR SUPERMAN TO SAVE HIM.

THEN THEY HAVE THE ROBOT.

I KNOW.

BUT, LEX, THEY'LL TRACE IT BACK TO Y...

I KNOW!

CALL THE CLOWN! I NEED ONE LAST MEETING!

...HOW COULD YOU HAVE LIED TO ME LIKE THAT?

NOW, I NEVER ACTUALLY SAID I WASN'T BATMAN...

OW!

YOU WANT TO KNOW WHAT REALLY GALLS ME? I MEAN, BESIDES THE FACT THAT THE NEW MAN IN MY LIFE IS REALLY TWO MEN?

SLAP

HERE I AM, SITTING ON THE HOTTEST STORY OF THE YEAR--"BATMAN UNMASKED"--

--AND THERE'S NOT NOT A BLESSED THING I CAN DO ABOUT IT.

THEN YOU REALLY DO LOVE ME.

OW!

I'LL GET SOME IODINE FOR THAT SCRAPE.

SLAP

BURNING, STINGING IODINE!

I SEE SHE'S TAKING IT WELL.

IT'S IRONIC--SHE LIKES SUPERMAN AND BRUCE WAYNE, IT'S THE OTHER TWO GUYS SHE'S NOT CRAZY ABOUT.

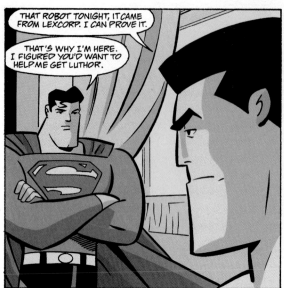

THAT ROBOT TONIGHT, IT CAME FROM LEXCORP. I CAN PROVE IT.

THAT'S WHY I'M HERE. I FIGURED YOU'D WANT TO HELP ME GET LUTHOR.

ACTUALLY, I'M HAVING SOME TROUBLE LOCATING HIM.

I MIGHT HAVE A FEW IDEAS. BUT SHE'S NOT GOING TO LIKE THIS, ME LEAVING SO SOON FOR ANOTHER FIGHT.

TELL ME ABOUT IT.

THAT BRUISE ON YOUR SHOULDER LOOKED PRETTY NASTY, BRUCE. I KNOW A CHIROPRACTOR WHO...

OH, NO!

HAS TO BE DONE.

I DON'T SUPPOSE A STERN BUT HEARTFELT LECTURE ON UNNECESSARY RISK-TAKING IS GOING TO SWAY YOU.

SORRY.

I DIDN'T THINK SO. JUST BE...

...CAREFUL.

LOOK AT ALL THE TOYS!

SANTA'S BEEN GOOD TO YOU, LEX.

HE MUST HAVE STOPPED CHECKING HIS LIST TWICE.

JOKER, WE'VE GOT SERIOUS PROBLEMS--

OOOH! A FLYING WING! TWENTY TIMES THE SIZE OF BAT'S AND, KNOWING YOU, LEXY, A HUNDRED TIMES AS LETHAL!

JOKER!

DID YOU BRING THE REST OF THE KRYPTONITE?

RIGHT HERE, CHROME-DOME. WHAT'S THE PLAN?

PAYBACK!

HEY!

WHAT?!?

WHAT'S SO FUNNY?

HA HA HA! DON'TCHA GET IT, HARL? WE'RE BEING SET UP TO TAKE THE FALL!

NO, SHE IS. I ABHOR VIOLENCE.

Y-YOU MEAN HE'S GOING TO KILL US?

HA!

Unghh!

NOW *THIS* IS FUNNY, MR. J. 'CEPT WE'RE NEVER GONNA COLLECT OUR BILLION BUCKS NOW.

TRUE...

BUT I SEE A DELIGHTFUL CONSOLATION PRIZE!

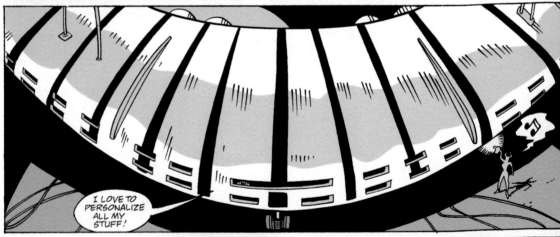

I LOVE TO PERSONALIZE ALL MY STUFF!

VERY AMUSING. NOW HOW MUCH IS IT GOING TO COST ME TO GET OUT OF THIS?

I'M NOT A MATERIAL GUY, LEXY.

NO, WHAT I WANT NOW IS FOR YOU TO KNOW WHAT IT FEELS LIKE TO LOSE EVERYTHING YOU HAVE, EVERYTHING YOU'VE EVER BUILT...

...LIKE I LOST EVERYTHING TO BATBOY!

AND SPEAK OF THE DEVIL...

HARLEY! WE HAVE INCOMING! BATS AND FLYBOY!

I'LL BE RIGHT IN!

BUH-BYE!

Ø'FL' % M

LUTHOR'S BEEN LINING HIS BUILDINGS WITH LEAD. IT BLOCKS MY X-RAY VISION.

WELL, THERE'S ALWAYS THE DIRECT APPROACH.

YOU'RE LEARNING.

A LITTLE DISTRACTION WOULD BE USEFUL RIGHT NOW, WOULDN'T YOU SAY, LEXY?

WHERE'S LUTHOR?

JOKER TOOK HIM IN THE LEXWING. HE SAID SOMETHING ABOUT MAKING LEX LOSE EVERYTHING HE HAD, EVERYTHING HE BUILT--

LUTHOR'S BUILT HALF OF METROPOLIS!

N-NOW WHAT?!?

GO AFTER THE JOKER. I SHOULDN'T BE LONG.

YOU'RE SURE YOU CAN TAKE THAT THING?

I DON'T KNOW NOT.

KRYPTONITE!

HA, HA! HOW'S IT FEEL, LEXY-BOY?

EVERYTHING WITH YOUR NAME ON IT'S GOING TO BE RUBBLE!

DON'T GLOAT TOO SOON, CLOWN.

YOU'VE GOT COMPANY!

BATMAN! IT'S ALWAYS BATMAN!

UH, PUDDIN'?

BWHOOM!

LEAD-LINED DOOR. I'LL HAVE TO THANK LUTHOR.

MR. J.! IT'S SUPERMAN!

WELL, WELL, LEXY! LOOKS LIKE YOUR PAL FLYBOY WANTS IN ON THE FUN!

IT WORKED BEFORE!

EEEE!

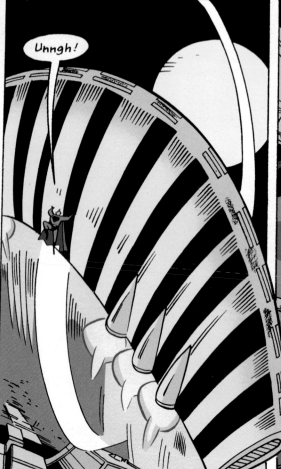

IT'S GOING TO BLOW! I'LL GET QUINN, YOU TAKE LUTHOR!

Unghh! CAREFUL!

Yiii!

Ungh! HOW DO YOU PUT ON THIS CRAZY...?!

WHOA!

HA HA HA HA

BOOOOM!

PUDDIN'....!

AT THIS POINT, HE PROBABLY IS.

HELLO, THIS IS ANGELA CHEN. WHILE THE COAST GUARD CONTINUES ITS SEARCH FOR THE JOKER'S BODY....

BILLIONAIRE LEX LUTHOR WAS AGAIN RIGOROUSLY QUESTIONED TODAY BY CITY OFFICIALS FOR HIS ALLEGED ROLE IN THE JOKER'S RAMPAGE.

THIS FOLLOWING ON THE HEELS OF WAYNE INDUSTRIES' SURPRISE DECISION TO SEVER ALL TIES TO LEXCORP.

AND, ON A LIGHTER NOTE...

JOKER ACCOMPLICE HARLEY QUINN WAS RETURNED TO ARKHAM ASYLUM FOR ANOTHER ROUND OF REHABILITATION.

I WANT A LAWYER! I WANT A DOCTOR! I WANT A CHEESE SANDWICH!

HA! NOW THAT'S FUNNY!

OWW!

I STILL WISH YOU'D CHANGE YOUR MIND ABOUT GOTHAM.

I ADORE YOU, BRUCE, BUT NOW THERE'S A LOT ABOUT YOU I DON'T KNOW...

MET AIR PRIVA AUTHOR

...AND I'M NOT SURE I WANT TO KNOW.

I UNDERSTAND.